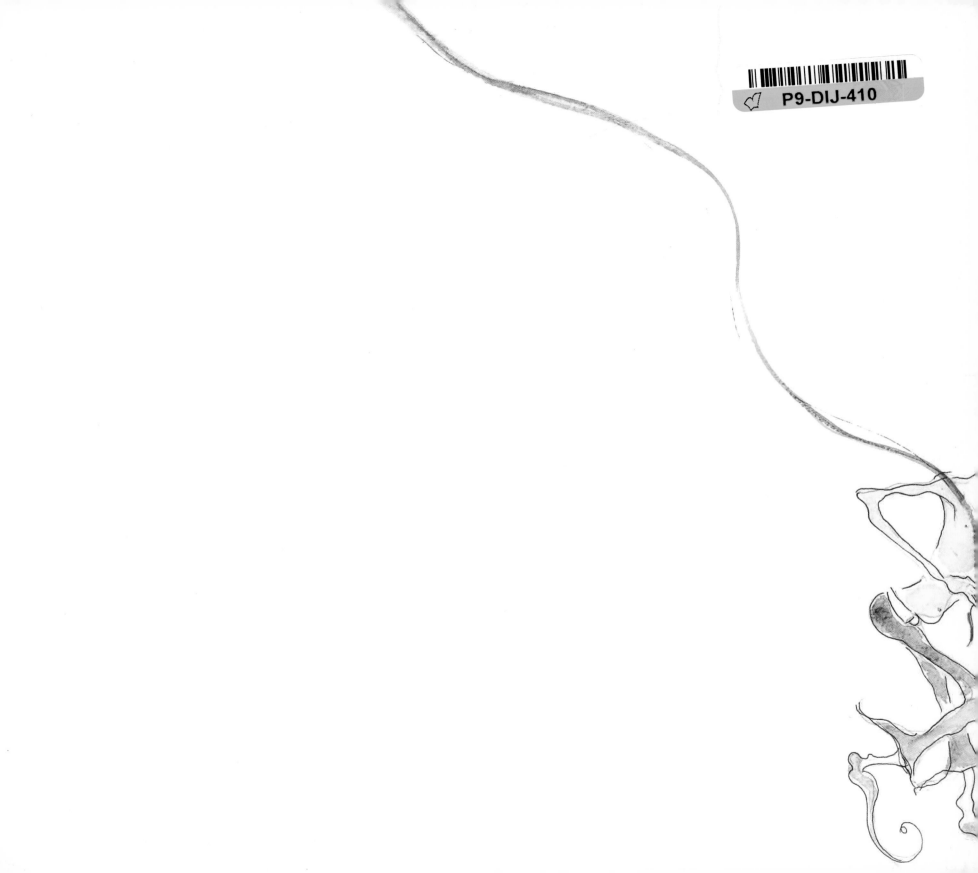

The Rainbow Weaver

Dear children and parents,

This book is unique in that it has been designed for very easy reading out loud. When each of the characters speaks, their words are in a different style of writing, so that you know straight away who's talking.

This is the sweet 'voice' of Tillie, our hero. She is very much like you or I - but maybe a little bit braver.

This is the deep, dark 'voice' of Hecatey the Hideous, our wicked villain.

And this tells you to talk in the three dainty, tinkling 'voices' of our delicate sprites, Skylight, Sunburst and Raindance.

If you are with friends and want to read our story like a play, choose a different character each.

What will they sound like?
That magic is up to you!

The Rainbow Weaver

Tillie's Tales of the Rainbow Realm

Daddy and Nathalie, for the rainbows they cast...
Mothers everywhere for the magic they weave

All morning it had been raining,

and Tillie longed for it to stop. Staying with Aunt Hattie for the week should have been fun. Her cottage stood at the edge of a wood that was said to be 'enchanted', and Tillie was desperate to explore.

Suddenly, golden sunrays burst out from behind a grey cloud, shining their beams through the raindrops to create a magnificent rainbow. A giant arch that shimmered across the sky, bowed gracefully over the meadow and poured down towards the stream at the end of the garden. Tillie gasped in delight!

It really seemed as if the end of the rainbow was only a hundred yards away.

Except there was something very, very strange about this rainbow. Very strange indeed.

The end of the arch… didn't end. It stopped cut-off, in mid-air, just above a bush at the edge of the river. As she watched for a few minutes, she was even more puzzled. The rainbow actually seemed to be getting shorter.

Curious, Tillie rushed downstairs. *"Back soon, Auntie,"* she called, racing out before Hattie could tell her to put a coat on.

As she headed down to the bushes at the river edge, the end of the rainbow seemed so close; the colours so bright… the air seemed dusted in magic. But then she heard it.

The cackle. An evil, nasty, deep throated, wicked kind of cackle. The kind of snicker that made your bones shiver and your hair stand on end.

Frightened, Tillie stopped short and ducked behind some reeds.

When she finally had the courage to peer through, she saw 'it'.
There, at the river's edge squatting on a tree stump sat a horrid, ugly hobgoblin
with a golden crown perched on his bald, scabby head. Every few seconds, his
bony left hand reached up and pulled at a thin, rainbow coloured thread that
dangled down from the short end of the rainbow. Tillie realised the thread was
tied to one of the two sticks he held in his hand. Every time he jerked down
a little bit of the thread, he wove the sticks in and out, in and out. Faster and
faster, chanting in a little rhyme as he worked.

"Rainbow colours oh so fine...
I'll weave your thread and make you mine...
A cloak of beauty really pure,
to make my powers truly soar."

Wide eyed, Tillie realised the hobgoblin was weaving a long,
magical multi-coloured cloak... from the thread of the rainbow!

"But look behind you," cried Tillie triumphantly.
He turned around, and saw his cloak shrunk.

"No... ooo!" he screamed in anger.

"No... ooo!

My magnificent cloak!"

Furious, he turned red, purple, green, yellow and blue.
In fact, all the colours of the rainbow.

As the goblin king chased her the cloak left a grey trail behind him.
But unbeknown to him, the robe was getting shorter and shorter,
the thread disappearing back up into the rainbow,
the arc getting longer and longer.

Suddenly realising what the sprites had done,
Tillie whooped with joy! She ran and ran, in and
out of the trees, the hobgoblin just missing her time
and time again.

Finally, as she circled back to the river,
he grabbed her wrist with his skinny,
misshapen fingers.

"Got you now,"

he sneered in a whoosh of foul breath.

Hecatey! *Wakey-wakey!"*

shouted Tillie down the foxhole. Within seconds
the tree stump flew open, and out jumped Hecatey,
furious he'd been woken.

He turned towards her, his cape glowing ever brighter
with the more colour it sucked in.

She started to run along the river back towards the rainbow as fast as she could. *"Can't catch me!"*
She cried, convinced that he could.

Raising his fist at Tillie, the hobgoblin set off in hot pursuit, not noticing the
thread of his cloak unravelling behind him. As he passed under the short arc
left of the rainbow, Skylight, Sunburst and Raindance swooped around like bees,
trying to distract him from catching Tillie.

As the rainbow unravelled further and further, the hobgoblin cackled louder and louder. Then Tillie stepped on a twig. Looking round with narrow eyes, he stopped his weaving...

Breaking off the thread with his sharp, yellow teeth, he threw the length of cloak he had made so far over his bony shoulders, and stared coldly in the direction of Tillie.

She gasped, turned and fled towards the enchanted wood.

"I'll find you soon, so stop where you are! You can't escape me, you won't get far!!"

laughed the evil hobgoblin. Looking fearfully behind her, Tillie ran in and out of the trees, deeper into the enchanted wood.

Racing through the bracken and over tree roots, she didn't see the strange, giant, rainbow-coloured dandelion ahead of her. Nor did she realise her leg had knocked its beautiful head… until tinkling music filled the air, and the fluffy spores flew

up and f l o a t e d

towards the tree before her. Then, Tillie couldn't believe what she saw. The branches of the tree moved like old, creaky arms, and reaching down the twiggy 'fingers' pulled open a hole in the centre of the fat tree trunk to reveal a tiny rainbow world within.

With the hobgoblin on her heels,

Tillie didn't hesitate. She dived head first through the hole, which closed behind her, and found herself rolling to a stop in a green, flowered meadow. Beyond it sat a golden castle with rainbow flags.

As she landed on the grass, unsure and out of breath, three birds flew towards her from the castle tower. But when they got near she couldn't believe what she saw. They weren't birds at all, but three exquisite little sprites.

"Are you okay?" said the first sprite, her pale blue wings fluttering anxiously.

"Of course she's not okay," chided the second. *"She's just escaped Hecatey the Hideous. Don't worry, my dear, we saw him chasing you. You're safe here. It's our home."*

"But who is Hecatey the Hideous and what was he doing?" Tillie asked, still upset.

"Why, of course, you don't know, do you? He's the King of the Hobgoblins. The ugliest goblin that ever lived. Cruel and mean."

"They say he picks the wings off pixies," said the third sprite, her golden dress beaming in the sunlight.

"… And the horns off unicorns," added the first sprite, nervously.

"As for what he was doing, we fear he's up to no good."

"No good at all,"

they all said together.

*"Let us introduce ourselves.
My name is Skylight…"*

The sprite with the blue wings curtsied. Tillie thought her dress the most beautiful colour she'd ever seen. Sky-blue pink with a yellow border. It reminded her of dawn, daylight and dusk… all at the same time.

Raindance wiped a tiny tear from her eye.

"I'm afraid we really do need you. When you're ready, just go back out and watch him."

"Follow him if you can, and discover where he hides," said Sunburst.

"We've tried ourselves, but his big nose can smell the scent of sprites whenever we get close, and he knows we're nearby."

"Go out and watch him?"

Tillie felt ill. Spying on a hideous hobgoblin stealing a rainbow was not something she wanted to do at all, but the sprites needed her help, and so she nodded in agreement.

"I'm Raindance,"

said the second sprite, her robe glistening with
hundreds of droplets, like a silver rain shower.

"And I'm Sunburst,"

said the golden sprite, rays of sunshine bathing her in a soft glow.

" We're the Rainbow-makers. Together we have the power to cast rainbows… but Hecatey the Hideous has been stealing them to make a cloak. We don't know why."

"Whatever he's doing, as he weaves, his power is growing,"

said Raindance.

"And we're getting so tired making new rainbows. We're running out of strength,"

sighed Skylight, fluttering to a stop and resting on a toadstool.

"What can I do to help?" asked Tillie.

They led her back to a giant curved wall of smooth
bark which opened at the touch of a wand, and helped
her climb back out of the tree, into the forest once
again. Nervously Tillie crept back towards the river... back behind the reeds.

There sat Hecatey the Hideous
(and he truly was). Talking to himself, he muttered curses
on the planet and all who lived on it. Tillie felt afraid.

"King of the hobgoblins, that's me,
ugly and evil as can be.
I'll make the world a dull, dark place
by stealing colour from the human race."

Tillie looked up at the rainbow… there was only a
little bit of arch left. At that moment the hobgoblin
stretched his arms and legs, threw the long magic
rainbow cape over his shoulders and took a few royal
steps.…

"It works! It finally works!"

he screeched, doing a little jig.

Hecatey cackled his ghastly cackle and sang a little song:

"A hideous joke? Not with this cloak.
I'm the dazzling king of the goblin folk.
I'll seem more grand when the world turns bland!
The most magnificent sight
in all the land..."

Tillie stared in shock. As Hecatey walked along,
the cloak seemed to suck the colour from whatever it
passed. The very air turned grainy. Trees turned black
and white, flowers and grass turned a miserable grey.
The land behind him was left ghostly and cold.

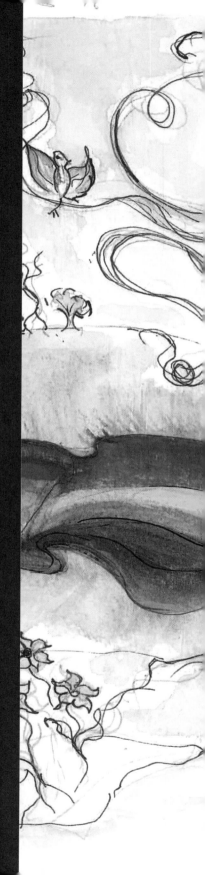

So **that** was his plan. By stealing the colour from everything else, he would be dazzling... **the most magnificent sight in all the land!**

Tillie watched from the distance as he walked close to her aunt's cottage. Her heart sunk as the colour drained from the once pretty orchard. Something had to be done. And done fast. She couldn't imagine living in a world with no colour. It was too awful to think about. Dark grey, light grey and more grey. And on a bright day, grey-grey. Grey flowers, grey balloons, grey parrots, grey party dresses...

"No!"

she cried.

Bravely, she followed him to see where he was going.
The hobgoblin finally stopped at an old tree trunk.

"Time for my mid-day nap... I'll steal the rest of the rainbow after lunch,"

he muttered.

Lifting up the trunk, he checked to see if anyone was
watching, then climbed down
into
its
hole.

Tillie looked over her shoulder, saw the sprites at the edge of the wood, and waved them towards her.

"It's worse than you think," said Tillie. "He's stealing ALL the colour from the world with the magic cloak. We've got to stop him fast."

"*Tillie...*" said Raindance

"*I've got an idea. When we give you the signal, you get him to chase you, and leave the rest to us.*"

To Tillie this seemed a terrible plan. But before she could say so, the sprites had slipped through a foxhole in the tree trunk and entered his dank, dark, underground cave.

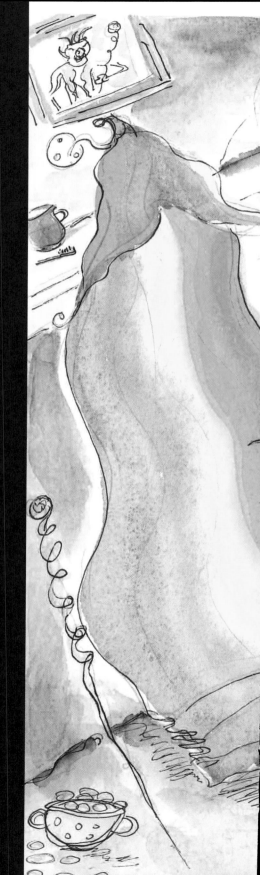

There lay Hecatey the Hideous
stretched out on a cobweb mattress, his snores so loud the
magnificent cloak hanging on a peg fluttered in the breeze. Very, very quietly the
sprites took the dangling thread at the end of the cloak and pulled it.

It unravelled!

Delighted, they hung onto it tightly, and flew out of the foxhole up, up into the sky. Higher and higher they flew, until they reached the remaining arc of the rainbow. Tying the thread back to the dangling line of the rainbow knot, the sprites waved to Tillie on the ground. Now it was her turn to help.

"Hecatey,